Balendu S Kumar

Things Just Happen

1st edition 2024

Font set from Minion Pro, Lato and Merriweather.

Cover design by Balendu S Kumar

CONTENT

Some situations can make you look like a bad person, but that doesn't mean you are a bad person, it's just an error in understanding. An error which will get corrected in due course of time.

Introducing Iva

Iva has always been recognized as reckless by the people who have lived around her for long enough. She wouldn't really listen to anybody; her mind would be set on something always. She would just zone out if the topic doesn't interest her. One could know this by looking at her eyes, it will be gradually shifted from the face of whoever is talking to her and will be fixated on some distant void. And out of nowhere she will zone in and she will have some reckless idea to share, though the context or the conversation so far might not match.

Last Friday she was having an evening coffee with her friend Sid in the restaurant. Sid was telling her that she should focus on the news value she is going to bring in rather than lose it over the emotional tracks.

"Iva you are taking things to heart, you shouldn't get attached to any of these. For us, the situation should be the column that we are going to write for tomorrow's news"

He went on like that for straight five minutes, and then he noticed that Eva has that look when she zones out. He clicked his fingers in front of her eyes and she was all bright with a broad smile, and started talking about how scared the neighbor lady was when she knocked her door holding a pan in her hand, which she bought on the way,

"I was going to tell her that I needed help as I got locked out of my apartment, but Sid, the lady only saw the pan in my hand and bang! Closed the door on my face"

"I felt shocked, but then I understood the situation that old woman was in."

Sid knew there was no point in repeating the paragraph he had just finished, and decided to go with the flow of the conversation.

"I didn't get you. What situation, Iva?"

" Sid, think about it in her shoes, I could have been some thief or a trespasser for her holding a pan ready to strike her. I feel now how fast her heartbeat might have gone up! I shifted recently, nobody knows me there yet."

"What about the locked-out situation? Did the lady help you afterwards? What happened?"

"Oh no, I waited for a few minutes in front of her door, knocked a few more times, and when there was no reply, I tried the next neighbour's door, and the family was kind enough to help me out. I had to buy a new lock though."

"You should keep duplicate keys," Sid suggested.

"I had them, but inside my apartment! My bad!" she smiled sheepishly.

"Well then, no comments."

He thought about switching to the previous topic, but then decided to just let it be. This is what she always does with everyone. It is unintentional though. She just has random thoughts going on in her head all the time.

A moment of courage can save someone, hopeless situations might hold some keys to escape, you just need to look for it.

Rescuing A Stranger

It was about to be midnight; Iva was scrolling through the feeds munching on wafers. She stopped scrolling when she saw a post about the moon having a halo tonight. She jumped from the couch and ran to the window, but she could see only stars.

It's not something you get to see every day. Although she was not keen on seeing the moon any other day in the past, today she felt like seeing it with the halo under the influence of a post on the news feed.

She decided to go out for a better view. The whole area seemed eerie outside, deserted and only lit with street lights, the neighbouring apartment windows were dark.

Anyway, it didn't bother her, she took a few steps ahead for a better view. Suddenly, the smashing sound of a glass bottle came from the right side. It was terrifying. In seconds, she ran and hid behind the parked cars and peaked above to see what was happening. Apparently, she was not the only one out there.

A man was holding a broken bottle in his right hand, he was swaying unsteadily. From the look of it, she figured he was a drunkard. There is a woman on the ground, petrified, tears rolling down, unable to scream. The man was moving ahead, and she figured he was going to stab that woman.

She was going to become an eyewitness for a murder.

No, no, this is not happening.

Her instincts were quick. She pulled the door handle of the car next to her, then did the same with whatever car she could reach in that parking space. The security alarms blared and filled the space.

She could see all the windows coming alive with light. The guy in panic ran in the opposite direction, dropping the bottle, but stumbled and fell on the ground.

People came out in minutes. Iva was already near the woman helping her stand up, and she explained everything to the confused neighbours. Someone tied the guy down and in fifteen minutes handed him over to the police. In half an hour, everything was sorted and everyone went back to their homes.

When she collapsed on the bed after the chaos, she remembered that she had forgotten to see the moon and halo! Well, the night was enough of an adventure. She was thinking about whether to write this news by herself for tomorrow's column, but then it would be bragging, so she decided to hand it over to Sid.

We have the tendency to create a mental image of someone when we meet them for the first time. It would do good if we could keep away the judgements and try to understand them with an open mind.

Clearing Suspicions

Iva was out in the park for a short jog, some sun can only do good.

There was this youngster at the traffic crossing who was waiting with her for the signals to turn green. He must be around twelve or less, sweaty hair, beads of sweat running through his red chubby cheeks.

When the lights turned green, they started running together and in the same direction. When they moved ahead like that, she started feeling the stress building up. It felt more like a competition, the kid was overtaking her, and she felt the need to overtake him and this repeated. The pace increased incredibly, it was becoming exhausting. The brat was doing no good for her inner peace, she badly wanted to shout at the kid for ruining her morning, but she knew it was partly her own fault not giving in and pushing for a competition. She saw a park bench and decided to break the frenzy. The kid looked back at her and grinned before running away. She ignored it and wiped her forehead.

From somewhere a Labrador appeared all friendly and cheerful. She gave him a head massage which he liked so very well and started licking her hands. The more she caressed the lab, the more she felt at ease.

“Is Murphy troubling you?” A quivering old woman’s voice resonated from above.

She looked up and recognised the women in a green cardigan as the one who closed the door on her face the other day. “No, no, he is super friendly.”

The old woman furrowed her eyebrows, seemingly recognising her. “You! The one with the pan who knocked at my door, what the hell”

She jumped up in a defending manner, keeping her hands up. “I can explain it’s not what you think.”

“Good lord you scared the hell out of me”. Granny responded with raised eyebrows.

“I’m your new neighbour, shifted here recently”

“Is that the way you greet your neighbours in your old neighbourhood, with a pan? Scaring them to death? Such manners, these new generation kids are wild”

“Let me complete, you misunderstood” Iva intervened. “I lost my key and I came to ask for help, the pan was something I bought on the way for my new apartment”

The expression of the lady changed to sympathetic, “Oh! poor thing, I’m terribly sorry for what I did, but I had my reasons, young lady, I got it all wrong. Come to my home this evening, Muffins for you dear for my sin”

“That is so kind of you, may I know your name?”

“I’m Margarita, and you sweetheart?”

“I’m Iva, nice to meet you Margarita. I’m glad the suspicions are cleared now”.

Random ideas may change your life if you choose to pursue them, anything that doesn't harm another being is worth trying, you will have experiences good and bad, embrace them, learnings will lead you.

The Pet Sitter

Murphy, after losing the attention from Iva, ran off to the park again, so Margarita left to look for him.

Rest of the time she spent walking in the park. She spotted two Poodles who were running in circle chasing one another, a Bernese Mountain dog lying beside its handsome owner on the grass, three Dachshunds in different spots walking with their pet parents. It was such a joy to watch them, more were there on the way.

"Yes, that's it" she fisted in the air and jumped up and down, a passer-by and some people sitting nearby glared.

She was struck with an idea. She texted it to her friend Miya, "Hey, I'm up for pet sitting, part-time!

In seconds came the reply "you upcoming poop picker, way to go girl...!!!"

"Yuck, hate you! Going to perk up my weekends, don't send anything else, I'm in a good mood!"

"Good luck! You do you!"

She slipped her phone in the pocket smiling and jogged back home.

It's for those brief hours I will get to spend with those four-legged lovable beings, even if no one pays me, I will be happy to just be with them. I may not be able to have one for myself because my living situation is not supportive, as such for having a pet. But this part-time pet sitter thing should end that shortcoming. She thought to herself.

She wanted to do something nice for Margarita. She still felt bad for scaring the lady, though unintentional. Considering her age, chocolate would not be a right choice. What about a wine bottle? But which one, white or red?

Probably, she will be making her own half-her-age-old wines. How about some special food? But which special food? Barely knowing how to cook for survival will not help in this situation. The cloud of thoughts filled her head.

She shook it off and decided it would be a better idea to visit the market, seeing some options would make it easier.

Window shopping is such a pleasure, walking immersed in the world of designs, colours and variety of products. She always liked that. She found a scarlet scarf; it would go with every colour and would suit the lady, she thought. Along with that, she bought a pot of lavender. It smelled so good.

The effort you put into knowing someone and the time you spent with them is extremely important, bonds are made over evening snacks and deep conversations.

First Cold Then Warm

How drastically some of those first impressions change when we get to know someone more closely. Iva was back in front of that door once again. This time she had an invitation. She smiled when she remembered the incident. She noticed the door handle now, it had a peacock carving in bronze, looked elegant, it suited the pastel-green coloured door in wood. It's strange a person fails to notice such details when one is under panic or tension. She didn't see any of this last time when she was there. Different coloured varieties of roses, marigolds and some other plants, names of which she didn't know, were tilting and dancing in the breeze on the veranda. She rang the bell. Margarita welcomed her inside. Murphy ran around her when she stepped inside.

"Murphy, don't trouble her" Margarita called out to Murphy. He became a good boy instantly and settled down on his bed in the corner of the sofa. The room had a classic look, with the shelf full of books covering an entire wall. The sofas were pastel green, wooden frames in dark brown with floral carvings. So many plants were in different corners and window sills. The curtains were beige, the glass windows had a view into the beautiful garden outside. Another wall adorned the shelves of wines. Yes, she has her own wine collection!

She handed over her gifts to Margarita,

"Oh, sweet child, the scarf is lovely, the lavender is perfect. I love plants. I have a lot of plants around here, but I did not have lavender, so thoughtful of you"

"My pleasure" she smiled and was happy to see she did a good job in selecting the gifts. Margarita went inside and brought a plate full of muffins. They looked fluffy and delicious. "Taste them, I made them. There are chocolate muffins, blueberry muffins and banana muffins. Blueberry muffins are not sweet, I can't have sweets, so I will pick one from that bunch, eat all the sweets when you can, enjoy life. Later, all of those sweet things will be taken away from you, advice from the wise and old" Margarita laughed while passing the plate.

Another one of her instincts proved right, Iva thought. All three types of muffins were soft, they melted into her mouth when she had a bite. Each had a delicate fragrance. The blueberry ones were a little sour as warned, she liked the chocolate ones more. She almost finished the plate while navigating through the interesting conversation with Margarita.

Margarita was witty and wise. Margarita had two daughters somewhat her age, one married off and another studying in college, both in far away places. Her husband died a few years back. Iva could feel the emptiness Margarita felt inside. Margarita had a way of bringing them back from any conversation that led to a dead end or an emotionally touchy part. She will bring up some funny Murphy catastrophes.

Iva informed Margarita that she was planning to do pet sitting and would love to have Murphy over at her place any time she liked. Margarita's reply was like "You have no idea what hell you are bringing your home. I am more than happy to leave him for a couple of hours. Don't blame me later"

she laughed and threw her hands in the air. It was indeed a wonderful evening. Iva felt at home after so long.

We cannot always be mindful and careful of things happening around us, we have the tendency to not notice something, forget something or may not be aware of something, that is perfectly okay.

The Book Case

Iva got a phone call from her last homeowner; she thought it was to fuss about wall stickers.

The wall looks like an empty canvas asking to make it beautiful, that's how she feels about bare walls. There should be something to give it a life, a macramé hanging some plants, or some wall stickers. The corridor wall had a sticker of five owls with big cute eyes sitting on a branch, as if they were watching and gossiping about whoever walked through that corridor. Her bed had a mirror opposite to it and the reflection on it was a cute girl freeing butterflies from a cage, the sticker she pasted on the opposite wall, it took a lot of time, the butterflies were tricky. Then some cute pandas above every switch.

But luckily the owner was okay with them, it seems. His call was regarding a book case she left behind. The book case was under the bed, that's why she missed it while packing. Now she needs to travel 120km to get it. A three-hour train journey, if the trains were on time, which never happens!

As expected, there was a one-hour delay. It was hot, there was nothing to do. She plugged in her earbuds and started watching the fourth episode of Lupin on Netflix. Then time just flew fast, she didn't hear the announcements, she didn't hear that her train had arrived, she didn't hear the commission of people. The episode finished, she came to her senses. She looked up and saw the train was about to leave. She ran with all her might and jumped inside just before the doors closed.

When the train reached the station where she needed to switch trains, she spotted the next one on the opposite platform. Again, she had to run. It was a little crowded, but she managed to get in.

She felt tired and started sleeping as soon as she sat down.

Fifteen minutes have passed, she woke up when there was a jerk. The view outside seemed unfamiliar. 'Is the train taking a new route, or did I forget the places already', she felt confused. She inquired the lady who sat next to her about the next station. Iva was in shock when she heard the station name, its in the opposite direction, that. That couldn't be a new route the train is taking. She told the lady where she was going, and the lady was bewildered and said Iva should have taken the other carriage. The train got split from the carriage behind, in the station where she boarded, and she was supposed to get in the carriage behind, and she got inside the wrong one!

It took an additional two hours for her to reach her actual destination after the whole adventure. It was past noon and a hungry Iva went to her usual dining place, which was a burger corner with vintage advertisement poster collections on the wall. Max was the guy in the counter. After retiring from the army, he started this shop.

"Long time no see, girl shall I take the usual?"

She smiled "Yes, the usual". She enjoyed the tasty fresh beef burger and sweet potato fries one last time.

The book case was dusty. It had those eight books, including her favorite "The Book Thief". It was a bit heavy, but she managed to take it back home. This time no wrong trains, so it took lesser time to come back.

Things might not turn out the way you thought, but finding ways to turn the situation in your favor is a skill that you should master. Learn what is going wrong and actively work towards correcting it

The One with Murphy

Margaret had to go to her younger daughter as she fell sick. It was an emergency. Iva got her opportunity to pet sit Murphy. That day she realized her apartment wasn't pet proof. Initially, Murphy wasn't happy when he saw Margaret living. He barked and tried to go behind her when Iva pulled the leash. Though it was their second meeting, Iva was still a stranger to Murphy.

To please and cheer up Murphy Iva gave him some treats, he was hesitant, he smelled them and then ate them at a go. He kept watching Iva with side glances. She tried to play fetch with him, but he simply watched and did nothing when she threw the ball.

The chaos started with the water bowl. She kept a bowl of water for Murphy to drink. He did drink it. After drinking half the bowl, he tapped on the side of the bowl, flipping it upside down and spilling water all over the floor. Iva came running and swoosh, she slipped and fell on the wet floor. When she fell, one of her slippers slipped off. Murphy was quick. He ran with the slipper in his mouth.

"Murphy No! Give it back! She yelled.

She got up, with one slipper on, and she walked teetering. Murphy was running around the room, causing a wave of disturbance to the still life around him. After wobbling for a moment, a coat hanger tumbled, knocking down a pot of plant on the way. After two rounds, Murphy decided to settle down and chew the slipper. When she tried to snatch it, he growled. She got scared and kept her distance, sensing a chance of getting bitten. He chewed her slipper as if it was a chicken leg, she sighed when she saw that her slipper is becoming tiny pieces. But it kept Murphy busy and the situation became calm. She went to clean the floor in the meantime.

The next victim was a pillow on her couch. In half an hour or so, the slipper task was completed, it was completely shredded. Murphy went back to the place where he had the bowl of water. She realized he was thirsty. She gave him the bowl of water knowing what he would do, and he did exactly that, flipped the bowl again after drinking.

“Bad dog!” she, with that disappointed look, cleaned the floor again.

Murphy went back to the hall, she went behind him. He jumped up on the couch, spotted the pillow, and gone! She tried to snatch it again, same reaction, he growled and she stayed away. She realized if this went on, her apartment would be empty in no time. She thought of the treats. She tricked him by placing the treats on the floor a little farther. It worked, he went for the treats and she got the pillow.

Going for a walk might save her apartment, she thought. It did work. Murphy seemed to like the walk outside in the park, though he was pulling her, giving her a hard time. But they got the opportunity to bond when she sat down on the bench, he became the good boy again, and she caressed him like last time. It felt good again.

We may put ourselves in situations that we find difficult and impossible, but take one step at a time, slow down and breath, you will do well.

A Week to Bond

While they walked back home, Iva got a call from Margarita.

"Hello Iva, how is everything going?"

Iva thought to herself to partially lie, or maybe it's not a lie because the walk went well. "All well, Murphy is a good boy. How is your daughter?"

"I am surprised to hear that. She has a high fever, and she fainted a few times. I'm worried. I have a favor to ask."

Iva could sense the tension in her voice. "How can I help you?"

"I need to stay here with her for a week. Could you take care of Murphy during that time? I know it is too much to ask."

The request from Margarita made her freeze for a minute. The entire morning mess flashed through her head. "Okay sure, my pleasure" her voice went high pitch on its own.

"I'm really sorry and thank you so much sweet girl"

Murphy pulled hard when he saw a female dog. That's when she realized, she was standing there lost in thought for some time. She suddenly felt too tired and as if her whole strength was washed away. She felt the need to sit down. She couldn't spot a bench, so she sat down on the grass leaning on a tree. Murphy turned back and looked at her. Iva whispered to him "This whole week you are stuck with me, you know that, be a good boy please." Murphy got closer and licked her face. She stroked his head, and it felt good.

She went straight to the pet shop. She knew she lacked pet supplies. First on her list was a proper dog feeding bowl with slanting edges which Murphy wouldn't be able to flip upside down. Dog food for a week, a proper harness, and then Murphy grabbed a chicken chew toy from the rack below. Iva got inspired to buy a few more chew toys and that's it, she felt ready.

"Let's face the music now!"

Margarita did not tell her about any commands to be used around Murphy. She thought of checking if something worked. She said "sit" a few times, he just stared at her, tilting his head sidewise, then she tried "come, fetch, down, roll, bark". Nothing worked, he simply stared her with wide eyes.

"Wow, you know nothing? Not a single word?". "Okay, shall we try learning? Will you learn?"

"Murphy come" She placed a treat in front of her, and he came running.

"Good boy, let's try that again" She went to one corner of the room and called "Murphy come." He came running again. They repeated this a few times.

Now Iva went to her room and called "Murphy come." He came running from the hall to her room.

"That's it, good boy, well done you learned your first word!"

Do not get caught up in the chaos, this too shall pass, stay true to yourself

The Office

The night went well. Murphy slept peacefully on the beanbag Iva had in her bedroom. But at 4.30 early in the morning, Murphy became the alarm. Iva had never seen that hour of the morning in her life before. But that day she had to wake up hearing the unstoppable barking. Murphy needed to go out and pee. She thought now she could go back to bed, but in vain because for Murphy the day had already begun. Now there is no going back to bed allowed.

At 8 o'clock, she got a call from the office insisting her to come to the office, otherwise it was a work from home day. She tried excuses but didn’t work. She finally told the truth about the neighbor having an emergency and having a dog at home for a week because of that. That too didn’t work, but she got permission to bring the dog to the office. Well, the office wasn't equipped well for Murphy either. They found out after a few hours.

She reached the office with Murphy. Sid was in the reception talking to interns, when he saw them, he turned to Iva. "Hey, you got a dog? You didn't tell me!"

Iva replied in a hurry. "Long story, will brief you during tea break, I need to see the chief urgently. Can you do me a favor? Hold him for a moment while I go see the chief."

"Ohh! no, no" but before giving Sid a moment to deny it, she slipped Murphy's leash on Sid's wrist and went inside fast. Murphy was not so comfortable with the stranger, so was Sid. The intern got scared when Murphy started barking. Murphy jumped at Sid, he panicked and let go of the leash. Murphy started running in the direction where Iva went. Now Sid came to his senses and ran behind him. People jumped out of the way, seeing a loose dog and causing a mess around, like tumbling waste bins, chairs, some laptops, files, all sorts of things flew in the air in the direction where Murphy went. Murphy did nothing other than run. The damage and chaos was caused by panicked people.

Murphy finally found Iva when she came out of the cabin, and he simply sat beside her like a good boy, and may be relieved to finally find her. Sid came to a halt panting, just behind Murphy.

"What happened Sid?" Seeing them like that, Iva sensed that something went wrong.

"Long story, I think everyone will get a break for the day now!"

Fair enough, the office was a mess, everyone got the day off to clean it up, and every emergency was shifted to work from home.

"So, the lady who closed the door on your face brought you more trouble! Wow, Iva!!"

Sid and Iva went to the pizza place after the office incident. Iva defended. "No don't blame her, it was a misunderstanding, how many times should I tell you? Besides, she gave me muffins, and it was my idea to pet sit!"

Sid made a face. Murphy was peacefully munching on a piece of pizza, as if nothing had happened.

Fear only limits you, when you face it head on you realize the things you feared are not as dangerous as you thought, but in fear you go blind and become unable to see the truth.

Miya

Miya was that one friend who was a constant, her schoolmate. They were in different colleges, then they were doing different jobs, none of those circles were common, but still the bond remained intact. You will have these circles due to social situations like a class or an office environment, where you will be having lots and lots of temporary friends who will become acquaintance and then distant over time once you are out and away from that environment. But that wasn't the case with Miya they bonded from a young age, and they stayed the same over the years.

That eventful day, Miya decided to crash at Iva's unannounced. Guess who welcomed her! Miya only remembers entering that door and then one bark and she was up on the sofa.

“What the hell, Iva! You didn’t tell me you had already started pet sitting! I thought that was a joke!”

“What a surprise! You didn’t tell me that you were coming..!! Murphy was an emergency”

Miya shooing and shifting around the sofa, her voice turned high pitch “Who is Murphy? Can you keep that dog away?”

“That dog is Murphy, he won’t do anything. Just come down, you are acting like a teenager”

“Can’t you see I’m frightened? Come here I need a hand”

Miya holding Iva’s shoulder, came down from the sofa, gripping hardly on Iva’s shoulders, she hid behind. Murphy now sat down and watched.

Iva kept him inside the bedroom and locked the door.

Iva shared the whole story with Miya over dinner.

“You did the right thing, but I can’t stand the dog. My sleepover is ruined”

“I’m really sorry Miya, next time I will make it up to you, adjust for this time a bit”

“Where does he sleep? Don’t tell me he sleeps in your room”

Iva looked sheepishly. “Yes he does.”

“Oh Iva, I am taking the sofa then, lock the room when you sleep with your Murphy!”

Iva chuckled "So kind of you"

Next morning, Iva opened the door without thinking much, she went to brush. Meanwhile, Murphy came out and spotted Miya on the sofa. He licked all over her face. Miya, half asleep, opened her eyes to the sight of a few sharp teeth, and screamed on top of her voice. When Iva came running, the situation was soothed on its own as Miya was frozen with fright and Murphy kept licking, somehow it made her realize he was not a threat. She stroked his head and in a few minutes they started playing. When you face your fear head on, you realize that the things you feared were not as dangerous as the fear itself. Fear limits you.

When you are on your own you wouldn't feel that you miss something in your life, but when you have good company for some time and then when they go away, you will feel the void.

The Italian

Miya stayed for two more days with them and then left with a lot of good memories. Margarita came back as her daughter was recovered. It was time for Murphy to go home. When Murphy saw Margarita, he ran to her and circled her, jumping and barking.

"Did he trouble you?"

"Not at all, he was a good boy. Initially we had some settling issues, then everything went well."

"Thank you so much for taking care of him, I have brought you some chocolates and marmalades". Margarita handed Iva a couple of packets.

"So kind of you. I taught Murphy some commands"

"Aha what commands?"

“Regular stuff, sit, take it, down, stay etc”

“Oh he knows them already, I forgot to tell you” Margarita replied.

“What? But he didn’t respond when I said them” Iva was surprised.

“He knows them in Italian. My husband was an Italian. He taught Murphy commands in Italian!”

“I see, I do not know Italian”

Margarita instructed Murphy in Italian “Murphy Sedersi.” Murphy sat quickly obediently.

“Murphy Vieni qui” Murphy came running.

“Murphy stringere la mano.” Murphy gave a shake hand to Margarita.

Iva clapped her hands smiling brightly “Wow that was awesome.”

Margarita laughed.

When Iva came back, she felt the apartment empty, she never felt this way before. She didn't feel so good so she decided to go grocery shopping.

The supermarket has never ending options, walking through those aisles, looking at different food is weirdly enchanting. Time flies by and you will never notice inside that place.

She saw that kid from the park again, he was pushing and playing with the shopping cart. Her mischievous personality kicked in. She rolled the shopping cart in the kid's direction. When she slowly passed ahead, the kid noticed. He increased his pace slightly. She increased her pace a bit more, and in no time they both started running with their shopping carts through the aisles. When they came towards the end of the aisle, she ran faster and then stopped suddenly. The kid did run faster but couldn't stop in time and hit the stroller hard on the rack holding bread packets. Bread packets flew in the air and rained on the boy. She winked at the pissed boy and turned to the next aisle.

When we see something, we assume, but what we assume may not be true, often what we see can fool us into thinking in a different way than what it originally is.

A Fool's Day

Iva saw a few teenagers begging in the street for money the other day. She saw the potential news value of the event. Possibly homeless orphans or children of drug addicts, helplessness that leads to begging on the streets when they should be studying in college. What will become of their future? She could bring some attention to the matter and bring some help for them.

Taking out her notepad, she went near them. She approached a girl in braids. She had a hat kept in front of her. She had a nose piercing; she had a tattoo of musical notes around her left upper arm. She was wearing an orange t-shirt and shorts. Three other guys and two girls sitting nearby had similar appearances with tattoos and piercings.

"Hi, I'm Iva, I'm a reporter. What is your name? I would like to hear your story, if that is okay with you". Iva started speaking to the girl with braids.

She looked confused. "I'm Vinni. What story?"

"How did you guys end up in the streets? Maybe we can go ahead with an interview. I will ask questions; you can tell your story by answering them."

The girl looked pissed. "Are you mad?"

Iva started her convincing act. "Look, I could bring serious help for you guys with this, if you cooperate."

"We don't need your help!" the girl tilted her head in the other direction, annoyed.

"Hey kid, I can understand what you are going through now, and how embarrassing it is. Don't worry, I won't put your real name in the article, you can trust me"

The girl started laughing suddenly, “Oh, this is so funny. I haven’t seen an idiot like you before.”

Iva was stunned by her reaction. “Hey, I’m trying to help you, and you are laughing at me, behave kid.”

“Okay, okay, madam reporter, haven’t seen a reporter reporting on a dare we took up on us at yesterday’s party, to stay the afternoon pretending to be begging on the street! Is that story enough for your article? Or is it too short? Do you need more details? I can explain the details of yesterday's party, it was so much fun.”

The girl continued laughing.

Iva couldn’t look her in the eye. “I’m sorry, I thought something else.”

She walked back without looking back. But she could hear the girl explain the event to her friends and an explosion of laughter behind her. She wished she knew the act of vanishing right then and there. It felt so humiliating.

Helping someone in need may bring back your sunshine.

Bitter to Better

Some days work may feel like a black hole from which you can't escape, too tired to do anything but a mountain in front. It would feel like the day was impossible. Iva thought of the day when Murphy came to the office and how they got a half day off. She wanted that to happen again. She looked at the laptop, the keys felt heavier to push down, the letters were reluctant to come up on the screen. The mouse pointer was reluctant to move. After a few clicks, everything was stuck. She closed the lid of the laptop and went to the coffee machine.

She thought for a moment whether to make the already bitter day more bitter with a bitter coffee. She kept the mug back and looked outside. Why not have something sweet? She decided to get an ice cream and a doughnut from the bakery outside. The combo might seem weird. She would break the doughnut into pieces and then dip it in ice cream and devour it. With every byte she could feel the stress moving out of her body slowly. When she felt relieved, she looked around. She saw an old man sitting at the corner table. He looked tired and distressed. A croissant on a plate in front of the person was neglected, he was in thoughts and looked at a distant spot. She walked up to the person, “Hello, if you don’t mind may I sit here?”

The person looked up. “It’s fine.”

“I’m Iva, I work in that building across the road.”

“I’m Bernard, I’m a retiree” he sighed.

“You look worried, is there something that is bothering you?”

“Well, I live in an old age institution. You know for some time now new investors have been showing interest in the institution and there have been some recent changes.”

Iva was puzzled. “Isn’t it a good thing?”

“On the outset it might seem like that, but these investments are purely business minded, expecting returns, they will improve the facilities, but then it will become crazy expensive and not affordable for people like me who live on pension. It’s concerning.”

“I might be able to pull some attention to this matter. I’m a reporter. I will write about this. Let’s see if we can stop them.”

Bernard smiled softly. “So kind of you, they are powerful people. Don’t get in trouble going against them for people like me who have only a few days left in this world. You are young, you have a future.”

“I believe it’s my duty to bring light to matters of injustice. This is not the first time I have went against powerful people. My weapon is pen, and I’ll fight with it for justice as far as I can.

Otherwise, however long it is, it will be a purposeless, meaningless life. I would rather live a short, meaningful one."

Bernard had a kind but surprised look on his face. "Be careful, and thank you, you are brave."

She felt a new energy streaming through her. She went back to the office determined.

Most of us see planning as a tedious work, but it is that initial workout or investment you need to do to have a healthy smooth life.

The Sticky Notes

She poured her heart into the piece and everyone liked the article, the matter got much attention. It was further pursued by a bunch of other mainstream media, so the investors were forced to agree on a fair affair. And a policy was made.

Her Chief Mr. Patrick was so pleased, he had always guided her in her career. Iva was unpredictable, impulsive and never followed conventions. Normally, people tend to follow trends, and they follow the unwritten rules involuntarily, like group consciousness. But Iva was different. Maybe it was that tad carelessness which made her that odd one that never followed the group consciousness. Maybe Patrick identified this trait of hers from the beginning, otherwise she would have been out of the office years before, for the same reason. Patrick was writing some sticky notes when Iva entered the cabin. He stood up and shook her hand, smiling. “You did well, that was a good one.”

“Thank you, Chief, means a lot”, her focus suddenly shifted to the sticky notes. “If you don’t mind, can I ask you something?" If she is curious, she must ask, the questions may be silly and the rank of the person doesn’t matter much.

“Yes, go ahead”. Patrick never discouraged anyone who asked him a question.

“What do you write in those sticky notes? You threw them away after some time, right?”

“It’s the daily planning, the things like what I want to have in breakfast for next week and what I should do to make it happen. If I’m going to have a salad for next Monday, I plan to go grocery shopping on Friday evening, then on Saturday I will nicely cut them and store them in a fridge. The vacations I will have in the upcoming months and the planning for them, things like that, I note down all the details."

She never thought this way before, she only saw the next thing coming and acted upon it, now she remembered those times when she started making oats and there was no milk, the time when half way preparing a pasta she realized the salt was over. "Oh Wow, that's interesting, do you think I can do that?"

"Why not, it is simple. You need to start thinking from future, what you want to do on a particular day. Then you need to identify what you need to do in the days before to make it happen. Note them down clearly. If needed, set reminders for them. If you need any help, you can ask me"

"Thank you, I will definitely try that. I was lazy, so I simply thought life is uncertain and restrained from making any plans, but now I can see the benefits". She grinned.

Patrick laughed, "Yea, life is uncertain, but still you can plan, so to a certain extent you can follow through and keep it in order. Rest, whatever happens, face it accordingly is my philosophy. Life will be much easier that way."

"Thank you, Chief. I need to go and plan for my next vacation" She winked.

"Vacation is okay but don't vanish without a trace for long, we need you here"

Find your entertainment,
wherever you are.

Sleeping Beauty

Iva kept her phone in flight mode. Dressed in pyjamas, she laid down on the sofa and switched on the TV. That was her plan for the vacation for a week. Being her lazy self, shutting the world out, doing nothing and relaxing in her home's comfort.

After binge-watching 5 episodes of The Queen's Gambit, she decided to get some sun. When she went outside and walked for about fifteen minutes, it started raining. She saw the clothing store on the left and decided it was the best way to escape the rain for some time.

You never know how time flies when you are inside a clothing store. Her plan was to stay until the rain was over.

The shopkeeper was a middle-aged lady, she was busy talking on her phone, and didn't even notice Iva coming inside.

Iva thought it is better this way. She don't have to see an attending staff asking her around what she wants. She walked around checking the price tags and the new arrivals. While roaming around she took a few tops to try out.

When she was inside the trial room, the lady, while still on call, looked at the time. It was ten past six, she kept the registers inside the drawer, turned off a few lights, took her bag, went outside and put the shutter down. Everything happened so fast. The shop was closed. But Iva was still inside the trial room.

When she came out from the trial room she understood the situation that she was in, she ran to the door and tried banging on it for some time, but it didn’t work. Finally, she came in terms with the reality that she is trapped now and nothing can be done. She sat down on the floor for a few minutes. Then looked around.

To pass time, she found the perfect activity, to try on the prettiest dresses in the shop. So, for a few hours she was trying out the most expensive dresses the shop had. She danced in them. She danced with the mannequins. She dressed up the mannequins as well, but the men's mannequins were made to wear dresses, and the women's mannequins some shirts and pants.

After a while, she got tired. There was this big box full of woolen blankets, under the 15% reduction sale board. She jumped above them and made herself comfortable among the soft fluffy blankets. She slept soundly.

In the morning when the lady opened the shutters, her site was a sleeping beauty on sale for a 15% reduction!

BALENDU S KUMAR

Balendu S Kumar, born in 1991 amidst the lush landscapes of Kerala, India. Now crafting tales in the heart of Germany. With an engineering background, she channels her creativity into story telling. "Things Just Happen" is her third literary venture. She infuses humor into her story telling, evident in the pages of her debut book "Berry". Her other book is Po-EM. Balendu, a traveler, photographer and writer, weaves laughter into her stories, inviting readers to explore life's lighter side through her lens and words.

www.ingramcontent.com/pod-product-compliance
Lightning Source LLC
LaVergne TN
LVHW040910150826
845672LV00007B/1975